Jennifer –

WITHER AND OTHER STORIES

BY SONORA TAYLOR

Ay '21

Good to see you at hearses That Care!

Sonora Taylor

TABLE OF CONTENTS

To Diane, a dear friend who loved horror.

WITHER

Katie sang to herself as she walked through the woods, looking for something to eat. She'd walked this path as long as her family lived in their cottage, the woods offering an abundance of berries, vines, and roughage to line their stew pot. Katie's stomach growled as she remembered her father's pheasant stew, made all the more delicious by crushed juniper berries and dandelion stems steeped in the broth. "Gives it something extra," he'd say with a wink as he sprinkled black pepper into the mix. Something extra to make her mouth water. Something special to share with her family.

Now she had nothing to share, and no one to share it with. Katie looked back at the cottage, a small dot at the end of a stretch of grass, like an errant pimple on a stretch of skin. Her parents hadn't walked with her in months, even before the hunger and illness that Katie felt within her had taken her parents away. They lay within the cottage, still and dead upon their mattress. She could still hear their voices, still hear them tell her how the city they'd left was worse than the woods. She could still hear her mother sing lullabies to her to help her sleep when she was little. Katie sang those lullabies now, sang them in a whisper to give herself a sense of comfort as she tried to live a little longer.

———

Katie had lived in the woods almost all of her life, but not long enough to completely forget the life she'd had before. The one in the wicked place, clogged with smoke and noise and the chatter of people. Katie remembered them in flashes, almost like dreams she'd dreamt as a child and carried with her in her teenage years. She mostly remembered them as nightmares, a nightmare her parents shared with her in their cramped townhouse. Her mother's textbooks loomed like towers as she prepared tests for her students, and her father's hands held dirt and the scent of brown paper grocery bags when he came home from his shift at the co-op. She even remembered her grandmother's hands, as little as she'd seen them. They often stroked her hair or gave her colorful candy, gummy bears that Nana said were good for her. "They have vitamins," she told her.

"What are vitamins?" Katie asked.

"Something good for you."

Katie took them, trusting that her grandmother, like her mother, would only give her things that were good for her.

Her mother didn't like the vitamins. She spoke of them the way she and her father spoke of the city they lived in: lacking. Unhealthy. Wicked. "You don't need those," her mother told her when Katie had asked if they could buy some.

"Nana says I do," Katie said with a fixed stare — her first act of defiance, something she didn't realize at five years of age. Her mother stared back at her with coldness, and Katie realized that she said something wrong. Her mother didn't speak a word, but Katie still felt a chill that settled on her heart and told her through its pulsing that to defy one's mother was to defy one's blood.

Thus, Katie said nothing more. She said nothing in the weeks ahead as her mother and father packed things in boxes and took them away. She listened in silence as they ate dinner and her parents talked about the lack of health in the wicked place, and how they didn't want any part of it. She looked out the car window without a word as they packed their final boxes and drove away from the city. Katie didn't realize until they'd reached the woods that she would never see the city or the people within it again.

The city, and their home within it, wilted in Katie's memory. She replaced those images with their cottage in the woods, replaced the scents of the city with flowers, bark, and fresh meat her father brought to their kitchen. They ate every day. They managed to stay warm in winter, and gardened in spring and summer. Katie grew used to the woods, and remembered that first year even in the second year, when she first went to bed with a growling stomach.

Katie couldn't ignore the growls, even when she told herself that what they had was enough. Her mother and father insisted that what they had was enough. Katie didn't dare say otherwise. She remembered too clearly the look on her mother's face when she'd asked for more of what Nana had given her. She didn't want to feel its effects again.

However, she didn't want to feel the painful hollow in her stomach. "Mom?" she called.

Her mother came right away.

"I can't sleep," Katie said.

Her mother sat on the bed with her. "Is something wrong?"

"Can you sing to me?" Katie liked to hear her mother sing.

"Won't singing keep you awake?"

"It'll help me go to sleep. Please?"

Her mother laughed a little, then began to sing. Katie's stomach interrupted her song. Katie worried the growl would upset her, but instead, her mother laughed again. "Are you a little hungry?" she asked.

Katie nodded. "Do we have anything extra to eat?"

"Not until morning. Not if we want enough to last through the winter."

Katie remembered winter in the city. There was much more food, boxes of cereal and macaroni and cheese bursting from their cupboards. Her mouth began to water at the memory.

"No matter what we have to eat," her mother said, "or what we don't have, we'll always have something, because we have each other."

"Will we have the city again?" Katie asked, pulling her blanket up to her chin.

Her mother chuckled. "You can't have a city. You can live there."

"I liked living there. We had more food."

"The city is a wicked place. And more isn't always better. Do you remember the plants I showed you during our lessons today?"

"The ones with three leaves? The ones I can't touch?"

"That's right. They're poison, and they spread their poison along your hands and fingers." Her mother tickled her, and Katie shrieked with glee despite her mother's tale of horror. "They spread when fingers touch the oils, and creep along your skin. The ivy crawls along the earth, growing even though it isn't wanted. Cities do what poison ivy does, and poisons more than just our skin. They poison the earth."

"With a rash?"

"You could say that. People can be just as pesky as poison ivy." Her mother looked out the window, her lips pursing as she thought of all the people she and her father wanted to keep Katie away from. "The earth provides us so much, and we respond by poisoning the thing that gives us life."

"And gives us rashes."

Katie's mother looked at her. "What?"

"The earth makes poison ivy, right? It poisons us."

"No Katie, she keeps us alive."

"So, she does both?"

"No." She chuckled, and Katie detected frost on her laughter's tail end. "The earth makes things which are poisonous. But if we know what to avoid, and how to care for what sustains us, then we'll be sustained."

Katie furrowed her brow, her mother's words ringing hollow in her six-year-old ears. Her mother clarified, "If we pick the right things, then the earth will do right by us."

Katie smiled. "Okay."

"And the earth will do right by us if we do right by her." Her mother smiled back, and a deeper passion flickered in her eyes. Katie flinched under its strength. "And she'll do wrong to the people who don't."

———

Their years in the woods stretched on. They almost never went to the city, and even then, only Katie's father would go. Katie sometimes went with him when she was little and she could fit in a bike seat. She loved the breeze as he sped along the trail connecting their cabin to the city. "We're just getting a few things the woods can't provide," her father always said when they stopped at the recycling center for old newspapers, a used bookstore for books on foraging, or the co-op for spices.

As Katie grew, it grew more difficult for her to go with him. She was too big for the seat, and too big for her father to carry both her and their wares back home. Her father told her many times she couldn't go, but one day, she felt an unexpected sadness when her father told her to stay in the woods. "But I want to go!" she protested.

"You're too big for the bike seat," her father repeated.

"Then let me ride into the city. I can ride a bike. I know what you need."

"Nine's too young to ride to the wicked place alone," her father clucked, though Katie detected tension in his voice.

"But —"

"Katie." Her mother's voice broke through them like wind through a field. She walked towards them and put her hand on Katie's shoulder. Katie could almost feel her mother's power creep across her back and spread over her skin. Her mother's control didn't scare her, though. It felt comforting, a feeling of nurture she felt when her mother sang her lullabies or gave her an extra piece of bread at dinner.

"Your father can go to the wicked place," she said. "I need you to help me forage."

Katie nodded. She and her mother gathered their baskets while her father left to get more newspapers. He brought less food from the city with each trip, for both he and her mother found more value in what they found in the woods.

Katie had trouble seeing that value when all she saw were leaves and dirt. "I'm tired of bark," she said with a pout as they walked down the path. "It's all we can find in the woods."

"Not necessarily," her mother said. She crouched to the ground and pushed back the branches of a bush. Katie gasped when she saw dots of red clustered in the grass.

"Wild strawberries!" Katie exclaimed.

"That's right. I knew you'd remember from your lessons." Her mother began to pick the fruit. "The woods will provide. We simply have to look for its provisions."

"What's a provision?" Katie asked as she rummaged through leaves on the ground, making sure to avoid any with three leaves.

"Something you need." She dropped the wild strawberries into Katie's basket. "Like this fruit, which will give you vitamins and make you strong. These are much better than anything from the wicked place, because the earth made them."

"Like the greens we had last night?"

Her mother smiled as she dropped more strawberries in the basket. "Yes, sweetheart. Exactly."

"Or these mushrooms?" Katie reached for a patch of yellow toadstools shining by a log.

"Katie, don't!"

Katie stopped even before her mother's hand grabbed hers. Katie looked at her. Her mother's hold softened, but her eyes remained frantic.

"Not those," she said, releasing Katie's fingers. "They're poisonous."

Katie frowned. "But they're mushrooms. We eat them."

"We don't eat those mushrooms."

"How am I supposed to know what kind we can eat? They all look the same!"

"Actually, they don't. The earth is very good to us. She tells us which mushrooms we should and shouldn't eat based on a variety of things. Shape, color, the list goes on."

Katie sighed. She was young enough to respect everything her parents said, but old enough to still grow frustrated by them. "And does the earth tell us what shapes and colors are bad?"

"Yes. And so do books — which is why your father brings them back for us. Let's go over mushrooms tomorrow for your lessons."

———

Katie was a fast learner, which served her well for her daily lessons with her mother. Learning quickly meant going back outside and finding what more the woods could provide, or setting aside her mother's dusty textbooks in favor of the newspapers her father brought home. Katie loved to read the papers from beginning to end, even when the news was sad, like when wars began in far-off cities, or when someone from their own city died of a mysterious illness officials had traced to her food.

Katie didn't want to be poisoned by food, and thus paid rapt attention to her mother's lessons on foraging. The expansion of Katie's wilderness studies was going well. She no longer reached for poisonous mushrooms or deceptive berries.

Katie also liked to see her mother's happiness as they pored over the science books. Biology was her mother's favorite subject, and she stroked the pictures of plants in the book as if they were growing in the dirt outside. Her mother pointed at a drawing of a lily. "That's my favorite flower," she said, her finger resting on its petals. "I haven't seen one in years."

"They don't grow here?" Katie asked.

"No."

Katie touched the painted stem. She remembered touching one before, long ago. "I think I remember seeing them all the time when I was little."

"That's because we had them in our garden."

"Our garden!" Katie's eyes shined at the memory. It had been filled with all sorts of natural delights, from lilies to tomatoes. "Why don't we have one here?"

"Because the forest is our garden." Her mother turned the page, keeping her eyes on the book.

"But couldn't we grow things outside of the cottage? Like lilies or kale or even marigolds?"

"No. In the city, we needed a garden to keep nature alive. Here, the earth does it for us."

Katie remembered the barren paths of winter that she and her parents had foraged without success for the past few years. She rolled her eyes. "When it feels like it, anyway."

Her mother snapped the book shut. Katie felt a chilled wind burst from its pages.

"It feels like it," her mother said, her voice a hiss that slithered across the table and wrapped around Katie's heart. "*She* feels like it, when she feels cared for. It's not up to you. Her gifts are yours to respect, not yours to command. Understand?"

"Yes." Katie was too hungry to argue. She wondered if her father's stew, a bare concoction of simmered bark and dried mushrooms, would be ready soon.

"Let me show you something." Her mother pulled another book between them, a biology textbook with yellowed pages and the year 1974 blotted but visible in the bottom corner. Katie wondered for a moment why her mother needed a textbook more than forty years old for their lessons.

Her mother opened the book, and showed her a drawing of a beetle on a plant. "These beetles are pests," her mother explained. "They destroy these plants, and at greater numbers than necessary for the natural balance."

"Do other animals eat them?"

"Yes. Sometimes though, it isn't enough — especially when their predators are hunted, or are shoved out by people cutting down the forest for their homes."

"So, what happens when the beetles aren't eaten?"

"The plants take matters into their own hands."

"How?"

"They restructure themselves so that they become poisonous to the beetles."

"They become poisonous?"

"Yes. To the beetles. They sense they're being destroyed, and not in tune with the balance of the earth. So, they attack their attackers." She scooted the book towards Katie, who frowned at its pages. "Neat, huh?"

"I guess — though that sounds a little out there."

"It's not. They're evolving to survive, and punishing those who interfere with the earth's ability to provide. It's resilience in its finest form." Her mother stroked her hair, and Katie felt tingles rain down her skin like shards of glass. "It's what makes nature so beautiful."

"Daphne, Katie," her father called. "Dinner's ready."

Her mother removed the books, making way for bowls of their winter stew. Katie kept the science book tucked under her chair, and took it with her to bed later that night. She opened the book to read more about plants, to see if what her mother said was actually possible. Her research on poisonous plants stopped, though, when she chanced upon drawings of a naked boy and girl.

Katie grabbed her lantern, shining it over the page. There were six boys and girls, at three different ages. She saw a child, a grown teen, and tucked right in the middle, a pre-teen. The book said the girl in the middle was twelve. Katie was ten — almost eleven — but she shivered as she realized her body was more like the girl at six.

How could this be? How could a life in the woods, a life filled with what the earth provided to her, leave her so small? Katie slipped the book under her pillow and turned off the lantern. She heard her mother and father murmuring in the kitchen. Her parents would make sure she had enough, even when the earth did not. As she went to sleep, she shuddered a little when she realized that thought was a hope as opposed to a certainty.

————

"Katie, Daphne! I'm back from the wicked place."

Her father grinned as he said the name, and her mother laughed. Katie rolled her eyes. As she neared her teenage years, each year with less food than the last, she only grew to doubt her parents; and this included how true their assessments were of a place that was supposedly bad for her.

"I've just got a few newspapers today," her father said as he lay them down on the table. "Seems a lot of people in the city have been getting sick. They think it's e-coli from the spinach."

"From the bagged spinach, they mean." Her mother rolled her eyes as she leafed through the papers. Scanning them, but never reading them. Katie wondered if she ever read them, or if she chose not to so she could keep believing everything she said.

"Well, you know what the wicked dwellers eat. It isn't real if it isn't in plastic."

"Why do you go into the city if you don't like the people or anything in it?"

Katie's father and mother looked at her in mild shock. "To get a few things we can't get out here," her father said. "Like these newspapers."

Katie folded her arms. She'd been hungry and bitter since she woke up, and both feelings manifested in her words. "You barely read the papers, and even if you did, all they tell you is what you already think: that people suck, and we're better off without them."

"We still need to be informed," her mother said. "The earth gives us food and life, but newspapers and books give us knowledge."

"Oh yeah, I got a couple books, too," her father said. He lifted two green books from the box. "Updated foraging books — at least, as up-to-date as the used book store had."

"Maybe they'll help us find some new food."

"Or maybe we could buy some," Katie said.

Her mother looked up, and her father scowled. "We'd never do that," he said, his voice rumbling under his mustache. "The food we get here is better than anything you'd see in the city."

"At least we'd see something there."

"Yes," her mother said, sharing her father's scowl. "You'd see people dying from the food they eat."

Katie rolled her eyes, which helped distract her parents from her stomach growling. "We don't have to buy spinach. But maybe we could buy some soup, or even some bread —"

"It all comes from the same place. All the food in the city comes from factories, factories that poison the earth instead of sustaining it. That's what makes the food rotten, and why that food gives people cancer or makes them vomit until they die."

Katie's stomach growled. It couldn't discern between cancerous food and sustainable food. It just wanted food.

"The food here isn't exactly helping," Katie said. "Look at me. I'm almost thirteen, and I still look like a kid."

Both her parents furrowed their brows. "What do you mean?" her father asked.

"I actually read the newspapers you bring home. I've seen the pictures in them, and the pictures in all your science books. I still look like a little girl. I'm short …"

"We're not a family of trees," her father said.

"I don't have breasts …"

Her father fidgeted, and her mother said, "Don't worry about your breast size, honey. That's a vanity you don't need."

"And I don't even have my period!"

"I'm going to make dinner," her father said, darting towards the stove. Her mother motioned her towards the bedroom. Katie sat on the bed, and her mother closed the door.

"Katie, why are you concerned about your menses?"

Katie sighed. "I should have it by now. Your science book says so."

"That book is for learning about plants, not your body."

"It teaches both."

"Well, if you looked at more than just the pictures, you'd see that girls typically have their period by twelve or thirteen."

Katie felt an angry, embarrassed burn settle in her heart at her mother thinking she was uninformed.

"You're only thirteen," her mother added. "And some girls get it at fourteen or fifteen."

"And some don't get it at all." Katie looked at her thinning wrists. "I don't think I ever will.

I have nothing that the book says a girl my age should have."

"Maybe not by the book." Her mother stroked her back. "But maybe you do by the earth."

Katie stiffened. Her mother's caress ceased.

"What's wrong?" her mother asked.

"What do you mean, by the earth?"

The caress resumed. "Everything you say you don't have — that the book says you don't have — is something related to fertility. Breasts provide milk for babies. Your menses provides blood for an embryo. They set the building blocks for more people." Katie looked up at her mother, who smiled at her. "By not having the means to add more people to the earth, maybe you have everything you need to keep the earth sustained. Everything you need for the earth to keep sustaining you."

Katie wanted to spit. She wanted to jump up, accuse her mother of being ridiculous.

Katie shrugged. "Maybe so."

She knew better than to argue with her mother. She was also too hungry.

———

Katie couldn't sleep that night. She kept thinking of her mother's words, how her mother smiled as she spoke of Katie not being able to grow. How she'd smiled at her with nothing like kindness.

Mothers were supposed to provide. If one cared for their mother, then one would be sustained. Katie listened to her mother, lived where she said and ate what she and her father offered. She was still hungry.

Her stomach growled so much that she winced. She looked outside and saw the moon was full. It cast a light over her bed that was almost as strong as her lantern. The cabin was quiet. Katie knew her parents were asleep.

She also knew how to ride a bike.

Katie crept outside and hopped on her father's bike. It wobbled a little with the first few peddles, but soon enough, Katie got her bearings and peddled down the worn dirt path connecting their cottage to the city. She wasn't afraid of the dark or the shadows of unknown animals scurrying out of her way. She was too determined to see the lights and buildings she remembered from when she was little. The memories were fading with each day she spent in the woods. She didn't want them to shrivel and die before she did.

The first streetlight nearly blinded her. She blinked and shielded her eyes as the dirt became asphalt and she entered the city. She didn't remember it ever looking like this. Lights dotted the roads, trees, and sidewalks like abscesses. Few people wandered about, but they were there. They walked in small groups or leaned against walls, trying not to be seen in the shadows. One woman leaned against a brick wall with her head in her hands. Katie looked away as the woman knelt down and began to vomit. She figured the woman didn't want to be seen.

Katie remembered a 7-Eleven her father often rode by with a scowl on his way to the recycling center. She rode down the street until she saw its red, green, and white stripes glaring up the road. There was a trash can outside overflowing with wrappers. She felt a rush of hope as she hopped off her bike. Wrappers meant food.

She walked inside and almost buckled over with the light. It reminded her of the way her mother's history books described bombs in far-off places, bombs that destroyed cities in flashes of light. Katie squinted as she meandered through the aisles. She noticed prices underneath the food, and cursed at her lack of money. She hoped the lack of people in the store would help her conceal a few snacks in her pockets to take undetected.

There weren't a lot of people, but they were there. Nocturnal creatures made all the harsher under the fluorescents. She saw men who glowered at cans of beer, women who frowned as they purchased gum. Their faces were gaunt and their fingers were shrunken. Katie felt uncomfortable as she looked at them, and wondered how the city could look so different from what she remembered as a small girl. Her father had said that people in the city were getting sick, but they didn't look sick — they looked close to death. How could the night transform people into monstrous creatures? How could the city cast such a shadow on those who dwelled within it?

Because the city is wicked, and so are the dwellers who live there.

Katie blinked as her mother's voice sounded in her head. She grabbed a few granola bars and focused on her errand. As she walked, she was stopped by a man standing in the aisle. "Hi there," he said.

She looked up. Another gaunt figure, with sunken cheeks and frosty eyes that peaked from beneath bangs the color of straw. He grinned, and Katie could see that his gums were red. He looked down at her chest, even though her breasts were small, as if to remind her that he knew they should be there and he'd leer at her anyway. Katie felt a chill seep from her heart and into her veins.

"Girl like you shouldn't be alone," he said. "So young and so pretty —"

Katie turned away and walked back down the aisle. She ignored the man's footsteps behind her. "You don't need to be alone," he said.

"I'm not alone," she replied as she kept her eyes forward. "I have my parents." And she couldn't wait to return to them, to return to the woods and escape from the wicked place.

"I've been watching you. You're here alone —"

"Get out of my store."

Katie and the man both turned towards the voice. She saw a woman in a red vest grab the man's arm. She had a diamond in her nose, one that glistened under the light. Something beautiful beneath the harshness.

"Leave this girl alone," the woman said. "Go home and take care of yourself."

The man spat on the floor before pivoting to leave. Katie saw that his spit was pink, and that it sat in a small pool of bile. The woman watched him until he disappeared out the door. She looked back down at Katie. Her cheeks were sunken and parts of her skin were ashen, but she didn't look monstrous. She just looked sick.

"Are your parents sick?" she asked with pity in her voice that Katie didn't understand. Katie didn't know what to say.

"Is that why you're here alone?" the woman continued. "Because they're sick and need food?"

"I need food," Katie said.

"I'm sure you do. Take it. Take what you want." She nodded towards the shelves of granola bars, then swallowed back a retch that crept up her throat. "It doesn't matter anyway," she whispered.

Katie was about to ask what was wrong, what she could do to help the woman. She wondered if the woman could come back to the woods with her, back to where she and her parents were hungry but not ill, in need of food but not in the clutches of the wicked.

Katie's stomach growled, and the woman sighed. "Just take them by the box," she said, before returning to her place behind the register.

Katie placed many boxes in the bin on the back of the bike. Her journey was a little slower from the weight, but it was worth it to get away from the wicked place and return to the woods with food in tow. Katie vowed not to waste it, if only so she wouldn't have to return.

———

"It's getting harder to go to the wicked place."

Her father walked inside, a stack of papers under his elbow. Katie darted to greet him, having developed a new fondness for the papers after her journey to the city all those months ago. It kept her connected to what was happening beyond their cottage without having to face it herself — and with each passing week, and each repeated headline of deaths and illness beyond the forest, she grew more grateful that she didn't have to face it directly.

"Maybe it's a blessing in disguise," her mother said, kissing his cheek while he handed Katie the latest stack. "It keeps us away from their diseases."

"Maybe so."

Katie couldn't help but agree with her parent's thoughts as she read through the latest deaths in the paper. People were still dying, and in numbers too great to trace to one poisonous crop. "It can't be e-coli, can it?" Katie asked.

"It could be," her father said, as he and her mother unloaded the remainder of items from his crate. "It could be a multitude of things. Mother Nature has quite the medicine cabinet when it comes to illness."

"Do you think she'll find a cure?"

"I think she already has." Her parents chuckled, and Katie shivered at the sound.

"It's all the better that we're closer to her sources," her mother added. "The closer we are to her, the less likely it is that her food will pass through the hands of man and, with those hands, be scrubbed clean of nourishment."

"And rubbed filthy with death," her father added.

Their words rang true with the food they ate, even with what little they found. The number of people dead grew with each paper her father brought home, people that stayed on the boundaries of the city and within the printed word. Soon, the printed word couldn't contain them. Corpses piled in the city, then past the city and into the country, and further and further until her father's cooking couldn't mask their stink.

"Those damn bodies are poisoning the food," her mother said, her face cross as she stirred a bowl of bark stew. There were no mushrooms that week. "Human rot is seeping into the forest and taking away its ability to provide."

"Even in death, humans are pests," her father agreed, sipping the last of his soup.

"Well, we know what the earth does with pests."

"We're seeing it firsthand."

They chuckled, softer than normal, but no less unsettling to Katie. She didn't chuckle. She didn't protest. She simply sipped her soup. She found it easier to just let her parents be. They were who they were, and they were also her parents. It wasn't her place to fight back, or reject them. She knew better than to try. They were there, and Katie left them to themselves, even when she heard her mother vomit later that night.

———

The woods seemed to hush as more people died. There were fewer plants, and no animals. Katie read in the papers that as people traced the illness to the plants, they began to eat more animals. They forgot that animals ate the plants, forgot that the plants' poison seeped through their flesh even when their hearts stopped beating.

Her parents forgot to bring the papers as they grew more ill. "You go into the wicked place," her mother said one day, her voice a whisper and barely heard over the sound of her father retching. "See what you can find. Just —"

"Follow the path, I know," Katie said. She left out her journey all those years ago, to keep a secret from her mother and to try and bury the fear she had at going back to the wicked place. But her parents needed her to go. They needed her to survive, just as she'd needed them. But neither could save the other from the earth's wrath.

Katie kept a stash of food under her bed, one that only grew in time with her parents' illness. She brought them papers, and books with natural cures, the only kind they would accept. Katie knew the cures were in vain. She watched in despair as her parents wasted away despite their rejection of the city in favor of the earth. The natural had turned against them. There was no cure. There was only time, time which Katie borrowed through snacks and water she consumed in secret.

Even the snacks of man, though, came from the earth's hands. Katie often cried as she nibbled on a granola bar and watched her hands grow no fuller. The food that humans relied on no longer sustained them. The earth twisted its nourishment into one of self-serving, offering food that poisoned the people who poisoned her. Animals too began to die, and so did the flora. Even with her own impending death, Katie couldn't help but feel sorry for a mother who would both poison her children and die herself if it meant she'd no longer suffer.

"Katie."

Her mother's voice flowed through the cottage like a breeze through a cracked window. Katie looked in her direction. Her mother lay on the bed, weak from her last round of vomiting. Her father lay breathless beside her. Her mother lifted a hand, reaching out to her daughter.

Katie walked to her. She sat on the bed, and held her mother's sallow hand in her own withering fingers.

"I hope you know," her mother whispered, "that even with all this ... even with everything she's taken away ..." She looked at Katie's father, then at Katie's hand, then back in Katie's eyes. "... the earth loves you, and does what she does to provide."

Katie kept her gaze and grasp steady. Now wasn't the time to balk at her mother's words, or roll her eyes, or flinch beneath her touch. Her mother was wrong. Her mother being right wouldn't have changed anything. The earth had already decided their fate.

She lifted her mother's hand to her lips and kissed it. Her mother's skin was more delicate than a leaf, and its touch seeped through her senses one last time. "I love you," Katie said.

Her mother stayed still as Katie placed her hand back by her side. She closed her eyes, joining Katie's father.

————

Katie didn't cry for her parents. She knew she'd join them soon enough. Her stomach no longer growled, but mewled in resignation at its empty fate. Even so, she looked under her bed to see if any of her provisions were left. All she saw were wrappers.

Katie moved like a slow-rolling fog through the cottage. She took a paper from the table almost as an afterthought as she went back to her parents. She nestled between them like she'd done sometimes as a girl after having a nightmare. Even cold, their touch gave her comfort from what scared her.

She knew her time was coming. She also knew she had time. She thumbed through one last paper, skipping the headlines on the front page about death tolls, parched cities, doomed civilizations. Katie knew all that without a paper to tell her.

Buried deep within the pages, though, were stories of the mundane — a sense of normalcy amidst the turmoil. Pictures of celebrities — the ones that were still alive, at least — shopping or walking their dogs. Politicians enacting what policies they could before all sense of government was gone. The elderly celebrating milestone birthdays. Katie couldn't help but feel a little better as she read those stories, even when she knew what fate awaited them all.

Katie turned the page and stopped, struck by a full-color photo of yellow wildflowers in a desert. They glowed like beacons in an otherwise barren land. "Desert Born Anew After Years Without Growth," the headline proclaimed. Katie read on about a desert that bore no plants and no life for decades, then was suddenly awash in wildflowers. Park rangers estimated the desert once bore those plants, and now, after years untouched, it had healed itself and started fresh.

Katie sat up. Nature had healed itself. The earth had started fresh. She looked out the window at the barren woods. Perhaps they weren't entirely barren. Perhaps the earth, having started anew, had begun to provide sustenance once more to those who were still there.

Katie was still there — and she was still hungry.

———

Thus, Katie left her parents in the cottage in search of something to eat. The earth was still there — weakened, and brackish, but there. Katie had to believe that, like the wildflowers in the desert, something lay beyond the choked grass and empty kitchen of their cottage. Something that would nurture her back into life. She sang to herself as she walked, sang the lullabies her mother used to sing to her when she was young. She closed her eyes as she remembered her mother's voice, when it had been stronger all those years ago. It still rang strong in her memories, a strength that seemed to warm her blood and pump her heart.

Katie tripped on a tree branch, and her mother's song stopped short. Her basket skidded away. She stood to retrieve it, then whimpered as she sat back down. She felt too weak to scream. Her knee screamed, clambering for her attention. Food would have to wait.

She examined her knee. It was scraped and bleeding, but not out of use. She looked for grass to wipe the excess blood. All of the blades surrounding her were choked and dried. Her blood gave them more color and moisture than they'd seen in months. She looked at the tree which felled her. The root stood gnarled and black, seeping through the barren grass and oozing from a rotted trunk. Its branches reached into a yellowed sky, like a spider's legs ensnaring a maggot. She remembered how her mother would look at the woods and say in a dreamy voice, "Isn't nature beautiful?" Katie smirked, and felt a tiny jolt of strength to heal herself.

Once her knee was dry, Katie stood up and discarded the blades of grass on the ground. She held her hand in front of her after releasing the grass. Her fingers were crooked like the branches above her, and her wrist was gnarled like the roots below. Both poisoned. Both doomed to die. But only one of them had doomed the other.

Katie looked out over the forest — or what was left of it. Decaying trees stretched into the beyond, an army of the dead that marched into eternity. Its branches waited for Katie with open arms. Katie blinked back tears as she looked through the thicket. She knew better than to move forward. The path ahead held nothing but death, a brackish bramble of roots to trip on and bark to disintegrate under her touch.

Katie grew faint, and held the tree trunk for support. The bark squished into her palm like a sponge, but kept its form long enough to hold her steady. It hadn't yet completely rotted. It hadn't yet lost its ability to nurture her.

She looked once again at the tree's gnarled fingers reaching into the sky. The fingers of the earth, who her mother was convinced would provide. Her mother had been wrong, and yet she'd been right. The earth provided life through death.

Katie wondered if the earth would heal herself once all the pests were gone. She remembered the story of the desert and its wildflowers. If the earth came back, if the forest returned to its green and nourishing state, there would be no people to witness it. The earth would be sure of it.

Katie smiled in spite of herself. It was almost charming, how stubborn the earth could be.

Katie no longer felt stubborn. She didn't feel much of anything, except a desire to sleep. She lowered herself to the ground and leaned against the rotted tree. Its flesh was soft, enveloping her cheek and shoulders as she curled against it. She closed her eyes, and imagined laying against her mother's breast, the gentle breeze of her mother's fingers running through her hair as she sang her a lullaby. Katie whispered in tune with her mother, smiling as she drifted to sleep.

NESTING

I looked through the window and saw a bird on a branch. She held a twig in her beak, prepared to make a nest. I watched her fly away, her wings disappearing into the deep grey sky.

I stayed facing the window. Squirrels skipped along the rooftop, leaves skittered across the ground, and I stayed inside, safe from the rain that started to fall.

The bird returned, and plucked another branch. I envied her freedom. Despite a world that was crumbling, she had eggs to lay, mouths to feed, a nest to assemble. A home to build.

People were worms, either plucked from the ground or removed by a steady stream of rain. I thought the rain would end by now. I'd thought that upon the first illness, assured myself that upon the first death. My assurances were soon washed away by a steady stream of footage of hearses each morning on the news.

Pluck! Another twig in her beak.

I stood up and moved towards the window, wrapped in a quilt my mother made me, watching the bird. Where was her nest? Where did she hide? What was her secret?

I didn't know the secret of those who stayed out of the hearses. All I knew was that I'd never gotten ill when I stayed at home. When my assurances failed me, I kept myself a secret in the home that kept me safe. Safe from any illness, and safe from anyone who sought to remove those they thought were diseased.

"We just need to be safe," the newscasters assured us. Footage of police cars replaced the footage of hearses. "They'll make sure you return."

No one returned. No one came home. No one bothered to nest anymore.

I pulled my quilt more tightly around me, and watched as the bird flew back. Instead of the tree, though, she landed on my air conditioning unit. She watched me, tilted her head, and examined my nest.

"Looking for a branch?" I asked, though I knew she couldn't understand me.

She blinked, then plucked a dead pine needle that had fallen on the vent. One that hadn't blown away all winter. One I'd never left the house to re-move. I was glad I'd left it now. It had a purpose.

There was a knock at the door. The bird jumped and flew away, taking the pine needle with her.

"This is the police," a voice said.

I stayed still, watching the bird.

"We're here to move you to a safer location."

I sipped my coffee.

"We'll make sure you're safe."

I pulled my quilt around me.

"We'll make sure you return."

The bird faded into the sky. I stayed facing the window, even as I heard the door crash open.

SMOKE CIRCLES

There was a dance party in a tent beneath the stars. Music pulsed under the canopy, and the plastic sheets that served as windows vibrated in rhythm with the arms of women and the hands of men. Wine flowed and laughter sang.

I left the tent. There were better things outside.

I stared at the stars and finished my wine. As the last of the Cabernet burned in my throat, I caught a burst of laughter and a whiff of smoke. There were revelers around a campfire. It crackled through the darkness of the mountains, but I could still see the stars above.

An empty spot beckoned me. I made my way to the flames.

"Have a seat." One of the revelers motioned next to him and scooted over. Smoke circled around his glasses, and lingered in the stray curls of his greying hair. He didn't need to move. I wouldn't have minded his touch.

I joined the circle around the fire. The revelers drank and smoked in each other's warmth. The fire bound us all in a searing thread. I saw wine and whiskey make the rounds.

"Want some?" a woman asked, offering a bottle of whiskey as she wiped her lips. I swallowed, felt the burn in my throat, and tasted the smoke on my tongue.

"Smoke?" The man beside me offered a lit cigarette with a nicotine-tinged smile. I smiled back and held his gaze as I took a drag, a demure way to touch my lips to his.

We passed the cigarette between us, its ashes dropping to the ground. The logs vanished into smoke in the sky. Both mingled as the harsh scent of nicotine fell into the cedar's folds, and the rank aroma of marijuana entered the fray.

I laughed and talked with everyone. Our vices were our joy, and leapt into the stars with each flying ember and each ebbing flame.

"Have a good night," the man beside me said with a smile. The fire had died, and we all bid our leave.

"Be safe walking home," the woman said as she tucked the empty bottle into her purse.

"I will." I walked up the moonlit path toward my cabin. Alone inside, I held my jacket to my nose, closed my eyes, and breathed in the scent of smoke.

WE REALLY
SHOULDN'T

Kelly paced while she waited in line, and clutched her laptop bag to her side. She fingered the strap, ran her hands along its surface as she waited to speak through a keyboard. She preferred to speak when cloaked in the safety of typed words and written articles. When she spoke without that cloak, people looked into her — and worse, they spoke back.

Or even worse, they spoke first.

Or worst of all, they spoke against the things she wanted. And when they did that, Kelly wanted to respond with things she shouldn't say. Thoughts she shouldn't have. Words that had no place at all, even in her mind.

"Kelly?"

Kelly looked up. A smiling barista held a white cup in her direction.

"One small coffee for Kelly?"

Kelly managed a perfunctory nod as she took the cup. "Thank you."

She walked towards a table tucked in the corner, away from the hubbub of drinks being steamed and office drones ordering jolts to get through the afternoon slump. A coffee shop wasn't her first choice, but her office was her apartment, and her apartment was being sprayed for bugs.

At least her computer could tell people to stay away in ways that she alone couldn't do. She sipped her drink and opened her laptop, readying her latest blog post. *Should We/Shouldn't We* had been Kelly's pet project for years, a haven for her opinions and the debates she often held in her head. The blog gave her a place to share those thoughts with others — though others often added their own points, whether or not Kelly asked for them.

Still, Kelly wrote. Her next piece was poised to be a good one: a point-counterpoint on whether using public transit encouraged green initiatives, or discouraged cities from keeping their character by bringing in too many outsiders. Her fingers ran circles around the keyboard, and her words fell in rhythm with cups being handed to thirsty customers. She paused only to stretch and crack her neck.

A voice in her head reminded her not to focus so much that her neck got stiff. "It puts you out of commission for other things," the voice whispered, hot in her ear as long fingers rubbed her shoulders.

She shook her head, and shook off the voice and its fingers. She had work to do.

She took one final sip, and was about to make one final keystroke, when that same voice said, "Kelly?"

Her fingers halted, the cursor beating in time with her heart as it failed to produce a closing sentence. She looked up, and saw who she expected to see. Even though it'd been months since she'd heard that voice — outside of her own head, at least — she knew exactly whose it was.

"Josh."

Josh smiled as he walked closer. He looked just like she remembered him — and like he hadn't changed or showered since. He wore a wrinkled white t-shirt, faded jeans rumpled over a pair of dirty boots, stubble grown for an exact number of days, and blond hair oiled brown, as it only ever saw enough shampoo to keep the grease to a minimum.

He always managed to look like a slob — and like always, to Kelly's dismay, he didn't look bad. His faded clothes and lack of grooming did nothing to temper his cedar green eyes or his smile, both of which came dangerously close to her as he stopped in front of her table.

"It's been a long time," Josh said. "How have you been?"

"I've been okay," she replied. She knew better than to give him too many details. "How about you?"

"Can't complain. Mostly doing odd jobs here and there." He cocked his eyebrows at her. "Are you still writing your blog?"

Kelly sighed a little. He always pressed for details — and like always, he managed to get them. "I am," she said. "I'm working on a new post now, actually."

"How about that?" Without asking, he pulled the chair across from her to the side of the table and sat down. "Working on the blog that brought us together."

Kelly couldn't help but smile. She tried to keep it as small as possible to let him know she smiled at the coincidence of it, not the memory. "Your comments were some of my earliest," she said. "Not to mention the most colorful."

"Hey, I liked what I read." Josh leaned on the table, which moved his arm close to hers. A warmth crept across her skin, bridging the gap between them. "And I really liked the author."

"Don't."

His smile fell, and she moved her arm to her lap.

"There's a reason we ended things," she said, her eyes on the monitor. "Please don't remind me why we began them."

"Hey, I'm just sharing a memory." He removed his arm from the table, and folded both hands in his lap. "Even if we're not together anymore, we shared a lot. We always will."

"Always did."

"Yeah, that's what I meant." He gave a half-smile. "Always one to use the right word."

"It matters. The smallest word can change a whole sentence. Sometimes a whole life."

"Like 'goodbye'?"

Her shoulders fell, and she closed her laptop. "Yes. Exactly."

"Josh?"

Josh and Kelly both looked towards the voice. Josh's eyes narrowed at the stranger who'd dare interrupt their exchange. Kelly recognized that look, the glare of animosity towards anyone who spoke to him without his desire. It was one she herself often gave — and one they never gave to each other. She pursed her lips to keep from smiling again.

The barista held another white cup. "Small coffee, for Josh?" The barista gave an extra-wide smile to him, one Kelly knew offered more than just the coffee.

Josh knew, too. He turned on the charm, and smiled back as he took the cup. "Thank you," he said as he raised the cup. "Thanks a lot …" He looked at her nametag, and Kelly saw his eyes take a side trip to her breasts. "Amanda?"

"Mandy," she said with a giggle as she tucked back a strand of her long brown hair. Kelly rolled her eyes. She knew it was an act, that Josh was doing this because she was watching him. She shuddered anyway.

"Thanks, Mandy." Josh nodded, then returned to Kelly. "Well, I was just passing through anyway," he said with a shrug, "so I'll leave you to it."

Kelly nodded back. "It was nice to see you." It was the truth, as hesitant as she was to admit it.

She should have known better than to admit it out loud. Josh smiled. "Would you like to have coffee tomorrow?" he asked.

Kelly blanched, but didn't say no. He added, "Just to catch up. It's been a long time."

She nodded. "It has." But had it been long enough? She wondered if it would ever be long enough.

"And the fact that I ran into you while you were working on your blog …" Josh smiled. "Well, maybe something's telling us we should reconnect."

"We really shouldn't," Kelly said.

"Even just to catch up?"

"You didn't say catch up. You said reconnect."

He chuckled. "I said both." Kelly rolled her eyes, but with a chuckle of her own. "But if you want to, we can keep it to 'catching up.'"

She shouldn't want to. She knew that catching up would risk reconnecting — something neither of them should do.

She pulled out her phone, and opened her calendar. "How about one o'clock?"

———

Kelly should have been writing. Instead, she was reading, with her legs stretched across the couch and a mug of chamomile tea by her side. All of her old posts were there, collecting dust on the digital shelf as their views stayed stagnant and their comments ceased. Looking through those old comments reminded her of the cruelty that the anonymous mask of the Internet allowed. Trolls peppered her posts with calls to kill herself, show her tits, or get a life. Even the more benign comments irked her, with requests to visit their own websites, misspelled thoughts on her words, or — her least favorite of all — suggestions on what she should say. "I'll say what I want here," she'd mutter aloud as she scrolled through their comments. "In the one place where I can."

Rereading the commenters' words reminded her of how lucky they were to be separated from her ire by a screen. But their words weren't the ones she was looking for. She scrolled and skimmed until she found it — a comment that glowed on the page despite the candle she held for its author having dimmed long ago.

You make an excellent point on knives. A cheesy opening line, but one that caught Kelly's eye nonetheless. She'd written a post on how frequently one should sharpen their kitchen tools. It wasn't even a question for her. She meticulously sharpened them once a week, wanting no interference as she carved through onion skin and tomato pulp.

However odd it might have been, Kelly felt a strange urge to answer the comment — and find out more about the person who wrote it. They moved from comments to email, from email to phone, and soon, from the phone to a date.

For all of Josh's talk about signs, Kelly wondered how neither of them saw it as one when they bickered on their first date, a cooking class that he'd invited her to. "You're supposed to slice the carrot on the bias," she said, taking the knife from him so she could do it herself.

"You're just supposed to slice it," Josh said with a frown as he placed his hand over the remaining carrots. "It doesn't matter how."

"But it does. It says so right on the recipe."

"As long as they're sliced, the dish will be fine."

"It affects everything: cooking time, evenness, presentation ..."

Josh snorted. "Presentation?"

Kelly glared at him. "Yes. It matters."

"Excuse me." Kelly and Josh looked up, and saw the instructor stare at them with pursed lips and eyes as thin as the strands of saffron on the counter. "Is there a problem here?"

Kelly and Josh narrowed their eyes, emanating coolness that widened the instructor's stern expression into one of fear. "No," Kelly said, keeping her reply quick in an effort to get the instructor to leave as soon as possible. "We're just having a disagreement."

"Which *we'll* settle," Josh added.

"Please ... try to keep it down," the instructor said. Kelly tried not to snicker at the way his voice stammered. "You're bothering the other students."

"Well, you're bothering us," Josh spat. Kelly turned to face him with wide eyes of her own. His gall was surprising — and exactly what she wanted to say. It was a bit of a turn-on.

The instructor regained his composure, and set his face once more. "Please leave."

"We will," Josh said, not even asking Kelly if she wanted to leave. He didn't need to. She wanted to go wherever he went.

"What an asshole," Josh said as the door closed behind them.

"Right? We weren't even that loud." She moved towards Josh's body to keep warm as they walked into the cold.

"Fuck him and fuck that class. Let's cook at my place — and slice the carrots any which way, *en bias* or in chunks."

"However the recipe says," Kelly insisted. He rolled his eyes, and she narrowed hers. "It does matter, Josh."

He smiled, and wrapped his arm around her waist. "All that matters to me is cooking with you."

Kelly rolled her eyes again, but with less conviction. She knew she shouldn't be charmed, but even then, she knew that Josh had a way of breaking through her constraints against what she shouldn't do.

———

The strength of his charm was only so much against the weight of her convictions. "We shouldn't do this anymore," Kelly said as she looked out his living room window. She didn't want his eyes or his smile to bring her back in, the way they had so many times over the past eleven months when she thought of ending things for good.

"Do what?" Josh asked. Kelly closed her eyes so he wouldn't see her roll them. "Make dinner?"

"No." She spun to face him, and her glare was tempered by how sad he looked, something he didn't hide quickly enough. Kelly knew he'd only joked to hide his sadness, but hiding behind jokes was a band-aid on the wound of their relationship.

"I'm serious, Josh," she said, sighing as she looked at the floor. "All we do is argue, and when we try to talk about it, all you do is make jokes."

"There're a lot of other things I do." He moved closer to her, and held her arms. "Things we do together."

"Things we shouldn't do together."

"Who cares if we should or shouldn't do them?" He leaned down towards her shoulder. "Just as long as we do them together."

Kelly closed her eyes. The things they did together were things she never thought of actually doing until she met him. Until he brought the thoughts she'd kept inside up to the surface, and all of them — all of her — breathed for air upon their escape.

Even with Josh, though, a part of her thought that those thoughts shouldn't be there. And they wouldn't be there, if Josh would only leave. And Josh would only leave if he believed that Kelly didn't want to do the things they did.

Kelly knew she couldn't convince him of that. She could, however, convince him of the one thing they did that neither of them liked to do with one another. The one thing that reminded them that they weren't, in fact, one.

"We argue," she said. "Is that okay, as long as we do it together?"

He stopped his descent. She kept her shoulders stiff. He moved his head back up, and looked in her eyes. "Do we really argue that much?"

"We're arguing about how much we argue. Shouldn't that tell you everything you need to know about our relationship?"

He smiled a little. "I thought knives did that."

She chuckled, despite herself, at her memories — the comment on her blog, their first date, and the others. Her voice caught as she realized their entire relationship would soon be a memory.

It needed to be. "I can't do this anymore," she said, looking back down at the floor.

"Can't?" he whispered. "Or shouldn't?"

She stayed quiet, and closed her eyes when she felt his lips brush her ear. "The distinction matters," he said.

She refused to be charmed by his focus on wording. "Both."

He sighed against her ear. "If you say so."

She did, and he reluctantly agreed. "You'll always mean something to me," he said as she exited his house.

"You will too," she admitted, pausing in the doorway. "I'll always think of you when I follow a recipe."

He chuckled. "And I'll always think of you when I don't follow directions."

Kelly stayed true to her word, thinking of him whenever she prepared dinner. She'd find herself holding the knife to the side, offering it to a phantom who would help her make the necessary cuts. The ache lessened with each passing month, but like a stubborn stain on a towel run many times through the wash, it never disappeared. It simply faded, living on in Kelly's memory as a closed chapter in her life.

Thanks to her having to work in the coffee shop that day, that chapter hadn't been the end of the book. Kelly set her laptop on the coffee table, then leaned against a pillow and stared at the ceiling. Months had passed, and Josh had only appeared in her dreams and memories. Why had she seen him today? What had brought him to her?

Kelly shook her head. They'd only picked up coffee at the same place, at the same time, and said a quick hello. There was no fate involved. That was Josh's thinking.

She sighed a little as she traced the rim of her teacup. That was Josh's thinking, and only a few hours after he'd been back in her life, she was once again sharing his thoughts.

———

"Josh?"

Josh grabbed their coffee from the barista — thankfully someone other than Mandy — while Kelly grabbed a table. Josh smiled as he took the seat across from her. He'd taken his second shower for the week, but otherwise looked the same as yesterday, save for the stubble growing a little further into a scant blond beard. Kelly tried not to look at his beard, or his lips. Instead, she focused on the coffee cup he scooted towards her. "Just a little milk," he said. "Just the way you like it."

Kelly smiled. "Thank you."

"So." Josh sipped his coffee. "How have you been?"

"You asked me that yesterday. I'm still fine."

"Even with me back in your life?"

"You're in my afternoon, not my life."

"You were always a terrible liar, Kelly. I know I've been in your other afternoons — and not just the ones we spent together."

Kelly looked down to avoid the net cast by Josh seductively raising his eyebrow. "I can lie when it matters — like when I told you how good a job you did cutting up steaks for dinner."

Josh chuckled, and Kelly returned her gaze to him. "I never believed you then, either," he said.

"Did you ever believe anything I said?"

"Yes, but the things I believed are things you don't think we should talk about now."

"I don't. Not really, anyway."

Josh smiled, and leaned back in his chair. His chest pushed against the limits of his shirt, and Kelly tried not to notice. She couldn't hold back the memory of running her fingers along its hairs, navigating the golden fields upon his skin and dirtying them with her sweat. She'd trace her fingertips along his heart, and spill secrets as he traced her lips and kissed her shoulder.

"Some of the things we talked about, though ..." Josh's smile grew, and she knew that he was reliving the same memories. She could almost see them running through his head, his thoughts coursing through her as strongly as they had when they were together. Back when they were so close to being one that Kelly had had to sever them back into two.

"Like on our third date," he continued, which snapped her out of her thoughts. He leaned closer to her. Close enough that she felt his breath on her cheek as he spoke. She saw the curls on his chest peek over his collar, and curled her fingers under her palm to keep from touching them. "When you told me —"

"Don't."

Josh chuckled a little. "You didn't tell me that. Quite the opposite."

"Maybe it's what I should've said."

"I know you don't believe that." His smile became sly. "Like I said: terrible liar."

Kelly smiled as well, her laugh coming out in a puff that sent the steam of her coffee flying towards him. "You're right," she conceded. "I don't regret saying anything I said to you, or any of the things we shared."

"Do you regret ending them?"

Kelly looked him square in his beautiful eyes. "No."

Josh looked at her for a few moments. His shoulders rose as he took a deep breath. "I wish you were lying," he said at last.

"Like you lied to me yesterday?"

His brow furrowed. "Yesterday?"

"You said you just wanted to catch up. All we've done today is talk about what we had." Kelly's eyes narrowed, her voice growing more cross with each word spoken. "And I know you're talking about that because you want to reconnect, even though you said that wasn't what you meant."

"Well Jesus, Kelly, I can't help it!" He sat back up, his eyes and voice losing all of their cool. "We had something. Something I regret losing every day. And maybe it should've ended when it did. But does that mean we shouldn't start over again now?"

"No," Kelly said, pushing aside her cup. She'd lost all of her thirst. "I should go."

"No, what?"

She furrowed her brow. "What do you mean, 'what?'"

"No, we shouldn't start over?" He stood up, but only to move his chair closer to her. To corner her in. Kelly didn't feel trapped, which scared her more than his maneuvering. "Or no, it doesn't mean we shouldn't?"

Kelly began to protest, and instead felt a lump form in her throat. Every memory of their time together was manifesting, reminding her of how much she missed him. How much she shouldn't want what they had together, or what they did together. How much she shouldn't want him — and how much she did anyway.

"I should go," she said again, lifting her purse.

"Should you, or shouldn't you?"

Kelly glared at him, which stopped his smile dead in its tracks. "Don't turn this into a fucking joke, Josh."

"Fine." Josh narrowed his eyes. "Though the real joke is the name of that blog. You know *Should We/Shouldn't We* gives the same answer, right?"

"What the hell do you mean?"

"'Shouldn't We' implies yes. Should we go to the store? *Shouldn't* we go to the store?"

Kelly stood frozen, trapped by a meaning she'd never considered before — and one she couldn't deny was correct.

55

Josh stood and leaned in close to her, his expression cold. "It's like Will They/Won't They. One is a question of happening. The other's a plea for it to happen."

"Who the fuck cares?" Kelly's exasperation grew harder to hide under the din of the coffee shop's noise. She saw a few people look at them, and longed to get away before they could interfere.

"Neither of them imply opposites." Josh moved closer, close enough to lower his voice. It only landed on Kelly's ears. "Neither of them say no."

She couldn't listen to him anymore, not if she wanted to keep the resolve to do what she should do. "Goodbye, Josh."

He gave a small smile. "That's not no."

"Goodbye." She pursed her lips as she swiveled past him, willing herself to not be drawn in. She sped down the sidewalk as the door slammed behind her. She wove through people heading back to their offices. All ignored her, which was just what she wanted them to do. What they should be doing.

"Kelly!"

Kelly stopped. There was always one who didn't ignore her. There was only one she couldn't ignore.

Josh approached her, and slowed when he saw that he had her attention. He stopped a foot away from her. It was still too close. It wasn't close enough.

"I'm sorry," he said.

Kelly closed her eyes. "Thank you."

"I'm sorry for what happened in there." He sighed, but stopped when she squeezed his elbow. He closed his eyes, savoring even the smallest of touches.

She removed her hand, and he opened his eyes again. Something told her to end it there. Something smaller told her to stay and say more. Though the desire to stay grew with each beat of her heart, she knew what she should do — even if it wasn't what she wanted.

"Goodbye, Josh." She turned to walk away.

"I found someone."

Kelly stopped.

"Someone else?" she asked.

"Yes." She heard him walk towards her. "Someone new. Just yesterday." His footsteps ceased, and she felt his breath on her neck. "Just after we met."

His fingers landed on her skin. She shuddered at his touch, the chill dissolving into tingles that bled over her skin. They pulsed through her veins and breathed new life into her bones.

"Do you like her?"

"Yes." His body joined his fingers against her skin. "But things aren't the same without you," he said.

"Aren't they?"

She felt him smile against her ear, and she chuckled a little as he gave her a kiss. "Come home with me," he whispered.

She leaned against him, sighing as his lips moved down to her neck. "I shouldn't," she said, with barely a quarter of her heart.

He turned her around, pressing his forehead against hers as he traced her cheek. "Shouldn't you?"

———

Kelly felt invigorated as they rode to Josh's place, kissing him the way she had when they were together. They were together now. They had to be. To banish him was to banish her. They needed each other. They needed to do the things they shouldn't do. It was the only way they could survive. She curled her fingers under his shirt collar, holding the fabric tight as the hairs beneath it tickled her knuckles. She didn't care if the Uber driver could see. She only cared about being near Josh again.

"We're here."

Kelly and Josh separated, and saw the driver giving them a pointed look. Josh smiled all the same. "Thanks," he said, giving a quick wave. The driver furrowed her brow, and Kelly giggled as they exited the car and sped to Josh's house.

Josh pulled her to him as soon as the door closed. He ran his hands up and down her waist, ran his lips up and down her neck. "I missed you so much," he whispered, his breath hot on her ear. He pressed against her, and began to lift her shirt.

"Where is she?"

Josh dropped her shirt, and looked into her eyes. "She?" he asked. "There's only us." He began to kiss her neck. "That's all there ever is."

"Don't lie to me." Kelly pushed him away, then began to run her palms over his body, softening him up to loosen his words. "I know she's here."

He smiled. "You know me too well."

"I should, after all we've shared." She kissed him, and gently bit his lip as she pulled away. "Where is she?"

He kissed her back, then moved his lips to her earlobe and gave it a gentle nip. "If you know me so well," he whispered, "then you should know exactly where she is."

———

"Tell me a secret."

Kelly and Josh lay on his bed, an empty bottle of wine on his bed stand. She'd spent the better part of the past hour licking wine from his lips, sighing as they spoke in whispers and touched each other with tongues and fingertips alike. It was only their third date, and Kelly already felt so close to him, as if the only thing between them was a layer of skin and a body containing their entwined souls.

"Any secret?" she asked.

"Any of yours."

Kelly laughed as he kissed her neck. It was only their third date, and already she couldn't fool Josh with her words. "What if I don't have any?"

He looked up at her with a bemused grin. "I know you have them." He traced his finger along her cheek. "And I know you're dying to share them with someone."

She closed her eyes. "Maybe they shouldn't be told."

"Maybe you should tell them to me." He kissed her lips, which broke into a small smile. "Maybe I share them."

He couldn't know that, but something told her that maybe, just maybe, he did. She kissed him, and began to whisper. "I love it when it's us," she said.

"That's not a secret," he whispered as kissed her back.

"I hate it when we're interrupted," she continued.

"Like that asshole at the cooking class?"

"Like anyone. By people on the street, by waiters interrupting us when we just want to eat ... I hate it when they're there. And I love it when we disappear together and cut them out of our lives."

"I love that too." He pulled down her panties, kissing a line from her shoulder to her stomach. Kelly gasped upon his touch, upon the possibilities that the two of them together could realize.

"But maybe if we brought them in together … maybe it wouldn't be so bad."

He paused, and looked up at her. "Brought them here?" he asked. "With us?"

"Yes. With both of us."

He smiled, and moved his fingers up her side as he returned to her neck. "I'd like that," he said as he kissed her neck. "I'd like that a lot."

"I would too." She pulled him close and kissed his chin. The stubble scratched her, and she relished the thought of licking her chapped lips the next morning. "Especially when we get rid of them after."

Josh didn't pause. He rolled on top of her, and Kelly felt his growing erection. "As we should," he whispered.

Kelly moaned as he slid between her legs. "As we will."

———

"Josh?"

Kelly narrowed her eyes. She recognized that voice. It had called their names before. "Seriously, Josh?" she said. "The fucking barista?"

61

Josh shrugged, and a devious grin crossed his face. "She was cute."

Kelly rolled her eyes. "You always went for the easy ones."

"What does it matter?" He gestured towards his bedroom door. "As long as they end up here."

Kelly smiled a little as she walked through the door and saw the barista on the bed. "Yes. Exactly."

"Who is that?" The barista looked from right to left, despite the blindfold obstructing her view.

"It's Kelly, Mandy," Josh said. "Don't you remember from yesterday?"

"What's going on?" Mandy asked as she moved her head back to the right. It was all she could do, since her wrists and ankles were handcuffed to the bedposts.

Josh walked towards her and traced his fingers along her chin. Mandy shuddered upon his touch. He removed the blindfold, revealing frantic eyes underneath. They sped from Josh to Kelly, a stray tear racing down her chin. "Did he get you too?" she asked, looking up at Kelly.

Kelly laughed at Mandy's mistake, and smiled when she saw that her laughter scared Mandy more. "I did," Josh said, a smile settling on his lips as he looked at Kelly. "And I couldn't be happier."

Kelly smiled back at him. "Neither could I."

"Please let me go." They turned their attention back to Mandy, who bit her lip to keep from crying.

"I won't tell the cops. I won't even tell my friends. Just let me go."

Josh stroked his beard, and Kelly bit her own lip to keep from laughing again. "Maybe we should," he mused. He walked towards the bed, and touched the keys on the bedside table. The woman's eyes widened further, hesitant delight flickering in her irises.

Josh moved his hand. "But maybe we shouldn't." Kelly grinned as she saw his fingers float down to the drawer. He opened it, and brought forth his largest knife. Kelly's eyes lit up, while Mandy's widened in fear. Josh held it out as he walked back to Kelly. She lowered his hand so she could kiss him without getting cut. Her lips met his, and she held him as close as she could, vowing to keep them as one.

"Let me go!"

They stopped. Josh pulled away, and turned to face Mandy. Kelly narrowed her eyes. She and Josh weren't one — not with someone else around. Not with all the others they avoided together, then decided together to take care of themselves. To sever them from their existence, breaking the others back into two — or four, or even ten, depending on Kelly's mood.

Josh smiled again, and looked at Kelly, raising his eyebrow as he held up the knife. "Should we?"

Kelly smirked, and took the knife from his hand. "Shouldn't we?"

"Please, Kelly." Mandy's lip trembled as the anger in her eyes flickered away. Scared resignation took its place, and Kelly almost felt sorry for her. "Please let me go," she whimpered.

Kelly walked towards Mandy, and knelt by her side. "I should," she said. She ran her fingers through Mandy's hair. Sweat slicked Kelly's palms as she gave Mandy a gentle caress.

Mandy closed her eyes. Took a breath.

Kelly grabbed Mandy's hair. She yanked back her head, and Mandy's eyes snapped open as Kelly placed the blade against her throat. "But I won't."

Acknowledgments

In 2017, I published a collection of short stories for the first time. I wasn't sure what to expect. I'd never shared my stories before, not beyond a few close friends and family. It was scary and exciting all at once. One year later, I'm doing it again — and as with the last collection, this was made possible by many people who I'm lucky to know.

I want to thank Doug Puller, who drew the amazing cover for this collection. I often send him my stories when they're in progress so he can draw a cover, and seeing his work from start to finish helped me see the stories through to the finish line. I'm always inspired by his work.

I also want to thank my editor, Evelyn Duffy, who once again brought incredible notes, feedback, and ideas to each story. The part of writing that I fear the most is revising, and Evelyn makes it a little less scary.

Thanks also to these stories' earliest readers: Tyrese, Julia, Illyse, Tara, Jan, and Nick. Your input was invaluable and helped each story immensely.

Thanks to all my readers, from the blog to the short stories to the novel. I love being able to share these stories with you, and appreciate you taking the time to read my work.

Thanks to my mother and father, for encouraging me every step of the way. From asking me to sign copies of my books to jokingly calling me Stephanie King, it means the world to have your support.

Finally, thanks to my husband, Will. I love you more than any written words could ever convey.

Photo by Karen Papadales

About the Author

Sonora Taylor is the author of *The Crow's Gift and Other Tales*, a collection of short stories; and *Please Give*, a novel. *Wither and Other Stories* is her second collection. She lives in Arlington, Virginia, with her husband.

Visit Sonora online at sonorawrites.com.